ABC Our Country

Mary Alice Downie
illustrated by Mary Jane Gerber

A
PIONEER
ALPHABET

TUNDRA BOOKS

First published by Tundra Books as *A Pioneer ABC,* 2005
First published in this edition by Tundra Books, 2009
Text copyright © 2005 by Mary Alice Downie
Illustrations copyright © 2005 by Mary Jane Gerber

Published in Canada by Tundra Books,
75 Sherbourne Street, Toronto, Ontario M5A 2P9

Published in the United States by Tundra Books of Northern New York,
P.O. Box 1030, Plattsburgh, New York 12901

Library of Congress Control Number: 2004117240

Library and Archives Canada Cataloguing in Publication

A pioneer alphabet / Mary Alice Downie ; illustrations by
Mary Jane Gerber.

(ABC our country)
ISBN 978–0–88776–961–0

1. English language–Alphabet–Juvenile literature.
2. Frontier and pioneer life–Canada–Pictorial works–Juvenile literature. I. Gerber, Mary Jane II. Title. III. Series: ABC our country

PE1155.D68 2009 j421'.1 C2008–908035–1

We acknowledge the financial support of the Government of Canada through the Book Publishing Industry Development Program (BPIDP) and that of the Government of Ontario through the Ontario Media Development Corporation's Ontario Book Initiative. We further acknowledge the support of the Canada Council for the Arts and the Ontario Arts Council for our publishing program.

ONTARIO ARTS COUNCIL
CONSEIL DES ARTS DE L'ONTARIO

Medium: Acrylic on canvas

Printed and bound in China

1 2 3 4 5 6   14 13 12 11 10 09

For Sofie and Nick, two little pioneers in a new century.
With thanks to Dr. James Pritchard, professor emeritus of history, Queen's University.
– M.A.D.

For Ted, Pat, and Beckah. With thanks to Yeshua.
– M.J.G.

A PIONEER ALPHABET

Who were the United Empire Loyalists who escaped to Canada after the American Revolution? They were farmers, soldiers, merchants, and people who lived in great cities like Philadelphia, Boston, and New York. They all wanted to live under the rule of the king of England, and not be part of the United States, so they settled in what is now Ontario, Quebec, and the Maritime Provinces. Most were of British descent, but there were also German, Mohawk, and Black Loyalists. Sometimes they came with little more than the clothes on their backs. Life in the woods was often difficult and lonely, but they worked hard and survived.

We live in Kingston, Ontario, which was settled by Loyalists in 1784. (It was first founded by the French in 1673 – but that's another story.) We spend summers, however, on an island in the Rideau Canal, in an old wooden cottage. Because there is no heat – except for a big brick fireplace – we don't go in there in winter. But as we shiver on chilly spring and fall mornings, when it is often colder inside than outside, we think of the Loyalists, who had to live in their log cabins through the long and bitter winters.

In spring, when we admire hundreds of trilliums, and on still summer nights, when we hear the coyote cousins of the wolves howling in the distance, the loons laughing on the lake, and see the fireflies dancing in the dark among the trees, we remember the people who settled here more than two hundred years ago.

Mary Alice Downie

A is for Abigail and Anna, my two sisters. Even though they are awful, I'm making them an alphabet book.

B *B* is for bandalore. I can do "whirlies" with it.
Abigail can only make it go up and down, and Anna can't even do that. **b**

C is for cranberries. We gather them in the marsh.
Mama makes jelly and sauce with them.

D   *D* is for dyes that color our clothes. Abigail nearly fell in the tub.
Now she has blue hands!   d

E

E is for eels that we catch in the river. Mama bakes them in pies. Ugh!

e

F is for fiddle. Papa plays by the flames of the fire,
while I accompany him on my flute.

F f

G is for geese that fly south overhead, barking like dogs.
Winter will soon be here.

G g

H   h

H is for hornbook that teaches me to spell.
I help Anna and Abigail with their letters – but not with their samplers.

I is for ice-fishing. The Indians who visit teach us how to do it.

J   *J* is for junket. We're going into town for supplies and, maybe, a treat.   **j**

K is for kettle, so big and so black. It hangs over the fire, cooking our dinner. Is it squirrel stew bubbling, or rabbit ragout with dumplings?

K   k

L is for log cabin. Papa helps build one for our new neighbors.

M is for maple trees. In March, we tap them for sap.
Then we make maple sugar and syrup.

M m

N is for nest. We find one with four new robin's eggs in it.
I wonder when they'll hatch.

N

n

O is for oxen, Oliver and Ophelia. Papa is glad to have their help in clearing the land. Anna and Abigail like to decorate their horns with wreaths of flowers.

P is for pigeons that blacken the sky. They fly overhead like a flapping thundercloud. Hundreds and hundreds of them.

P   p

Q is for quilts that Mama makes for our beds.
She uses quantities of our old clothes.

R *R* is for raccoons that race around, raiding our root cellar. What rascals! **r**

S is for soap-making, spinning, and stumping –
so much work for everyone.

S   S

T is for trilliums, which bloom in the woods like a carpet of stars.

U is for the uniform Papa wore when he fought for the king.
Sometimes he lets me wear it!

U U

V is for vines of wild grapes and roses.
They grow near our vegetable garden.

V

V

W

W

W is for wolves that howl in the night.
Anna and Abigail are frightened and cry. I whistle to cheer us up.

X is for exhaustion at the end of the day.
Mama and Papa are so tired that we play with Xerxes.

Y is for yarn that Mama spins into our clothes.
She has promised to make me a yellow waistcoat.

Y y

Z is for Zebediah. That's me. And Zacharias. That's him.

A Like other pioneer children, the twins, Abigail and Anna, lived in a log cabin in the woods with their family and household pet – Xerxes the cat. They didn't go to school, nor did they have television, computer games, or friends nearby. But even though they had many chores, they still managed to have fun – and get into trouble!

B Bandalore is the old name for "yo-yo," which was invented over two thousand years ago, possibly in Ancient Greece. Yo-yo's have been made of terra-cotta, silver, gold, horn, and wood. In the past, adults liked to play with them too. In 1985, a yellow plastic yo-yo was taken up in the space shuttle *Discovery*, as part of an experiment with "Toys in Space."

C Many early travelers kept diaries, describing what life was like in the "New World" in the eighteenth century. Mrs. Elizabeth Simcoe (1762–1850), wife of John Graves Simcoe, the first Lieutenant-Governor of Upper Canada, kept some of the most interesting. In 1793, she wrote: "The Indians bring us Cranberries in Spring & Autumn which are as large as Cherries & very good, the best grow under water. They also supply us with Chestnuts which they roast in a manner that makes them particularly good."

D The pioneers used dried leaves, flowers, and tree bark to dye their garments and yarn. They needed to wash and dry the yarn before steeping it in the dye tub. Butternut husks and sumac blossoms made *brown,* onion skins and goldenrod made *yellow,* and indigo plants or blueberries made *blue.* Then they washed and dried the yarn again before weaving it into cloth.

E They may look like snakes, but eels are really long fish with smooth, slimy skin. Although the Loyalists were given supplies for the first three years in the Canadian wilderness – pork, a little beef, flour, butter, salt, seed, and tools – they were expected to grow their own crops and vegetables. They also hunted for game and fish, such as eels. Luckily, both were plentiful. But in 1787, the crops failed, and some pioneers starved during what became known as the Hungry Year. Some had to live on leaves, bark, wild berries, and plants.

F Two hundred years ago, the pioneers provided their own entertainment, and musical instruments such as fiddles were often part of it. Children spun wooden tops, or played card games or jacks. Anna and Abigail might have played cat's cradle – a game in which a long piece of yarn is looped in a pattern on the fingers of one person and passed to the fingers of another to form a different pattern. They might have made shadow puppets, or told riddles or ghost stories by the fire, cracking nuts or popping corn in a spider (a cast-iron frying pan or skillet).

G One of the exciting spectacles in the Canadian fall is the sight of geese flying south in their great V-formation. Sometimes, clouds of smaller birds swirl down for a snack before heading south too. The pioneers used the geese for food. They made pillows and even beds from their feathers and pens from their quills.

H The hornbook was used to teach children to read and do arithmetic. A sheet of parchment or paper – with letters, numbers, and verses – was usually fastened or glued to a wooden paddle and protected by a sheet of transparent cow or ox horn. Little girls learned their embroidery stitches by making samplers, which also had letters, numbers, and mottoes, as well as pictures of animals, flowers, and fruit. Each sampler contained the name and age of the girl who made it and the date it was completed. Some were very beautiful and today you can find them in museums.

I Mrs. Simcoe described ice-fishing in her diaries: "The Indians have cut holes in the Ice, over which they spread a Blanket on poles & they sit under the shed, moving a wooden Fish hung to a line in the water by way of attracting the living fish, which they spear with great dexterity when they approach. . . . they were catching Maskalonge (a superior kind of Pike) and Pickerell."

J "Junket" is a word meaning trip or journey. Pioneers traveled through the woods along a "corduroy" road, which was made of logs and very bumpy! The logs rotted, horses got their hooves caught in the spaces, and passengers were often badly jolted or thrown into the mud. If they lived near the water, they could travel by canoe or bateau (a big boat with flared sides and a flat bottom). In winter, they traveled by sleigh, wrapped in bearskin rugs.

K The Loyalists cooked their food over the fire in heavy cast-iron pots and kettles. They had even baked bread, and though it would have had a beautiful brown crust, it might have tasted soggy inside. Everything was cooked in these utensils – boiled corn, pork, potatoes, and wild rice, which they were given by the Indians.

L The pioneers had to clear a space in the woods by chopping down trees with their axes. Then they would use the wood to build their first house, often a small dark shanty with a dirt floor and a blanket for a door. The Loyalists brought the idea of "bees" with them from the States. (In New Brunswick, they were called frolics.) A person would "call" a bee to help with clearing land, building fences, raising a barn, or building a bigger house. Lots of food – and whiskey – had to be provided. Women had quilting, sewing, and spinning bees, but children liked apple-pairing or corn-husking bees the best.

M Like so much else, the pioneers were taught how to make maple syrup by the Indians. According to Mrs. Simcoe: "a hot Sun & frosty nights causes the sap to flow most. Slits are cut in the bark of the Trees & wooden Troughs set under the Tree into which the Sap clear water – runs. It is collected from a number of Trees & boiled in large Kettles till it becomes of a hard consistence." Children loved sugar-making and came to the sugar bush with big spoons or ladles, ready to eat!

N Birds don't always nest in trees. The loon builds its nest as soon as the ice melts, close to the water, perhaps in a half-buried log or swampy marsh. It makes the nest from whatever is handy – needles, grass, moss, or leaves. The great blue heron is more sociable and nests in a large colony high in the treetops, on islands, or in wooden swamps. (Every summer, a little phoebe makes a very messy nest of mud and twigs in the corner of the roof of the veranda at our cottage!)

O Oxen were often used by the pioneers because they were cheaper to buy than horses and easier to handle on rough ground. They cleared land by drawing plows and dragging away logs. They also pulled wagons and carts. They were not guided by reins, but by a pole. Oxen were very slow, but if the plow got caught in a rock or roots, they would stand and wait patiently until it was freed.

P Pigeons have stout bodies, short legs, and smooth plumage. Passenger pigeons (migratory pigeons that are now extinct) were not used to people as pigeons are today. They flew so low that they could be knocked down by a pole! The last one, known as Martha, died in the Cincinnati Zoo in 1944.

Q Made of scraps of material sewn together, with padding in the middle to make them warm, quilts are really works of art. Some of the heirlooms are very valuable and passed from generation to generation. The patterns have names like Hen and Chickens, Bear Paw, and Log Cabin. Sometimes there is no pattern at all, and then it is called a Crazy Quilt.

R Raccoons live in hollow trees, burrows, buildings – or your attic. They have bushy ringed tails and black masks around their eyes, which make them look like bandits. They have a varied diet, including small animals, fruits, and nuts, but these mischievous creatures steal anything they can lay their paws on. They would certainly be interested in the contents of a root cellar, where the pioneers stored their winter vegetables.

S Soap was made by boiling a mixture of hardwood ashes and grease. Even animal bones were added and cooked down, and the residue placed in molds. Soap-making had to be done outside because it was very smelly. Spinning yarn or thread was done on a small hand-driven or foot-driven machine. Stumping was what pioneers did after trees had been cut down. Often the first crops were sown around the stumps, but the wood eventually rotted so they might have chopped them out or dragged them out with oxen.

T Members of the lily family, trilliums have erect stems bearing whorls of three dark green leaves and large single flowers. They bloom in the spring and are found in woodland areas and thickets. These snow white and sometimes red beauties were called moose-flowers in Nova Scotia, perhaps because they grew where the moose liked to forage.

U During the American Revolution, British troops wore red coats and became known as Lobsterbacks. Men in early Loyalist units often wore their ordinary clothes, with armbands and cockades (knots of ribbons or leather worn as badges), to show their loyalty to the king. Later, when cloth for uniforms was sent over from Britain, members of many Loyalist units wore red coats, but also blue or green.

V Pioneers planted many of the same kinds of vegetables we eat today, such as cabbages, corn, celery, and carrots. Their diets also included items found growing in the woods: wild grapes in juice and jellies, wild rose hips in syrups. In New Brunswick, the Loyalists survived mostly on herbs gathered in the marshes in spring: "sandfire" (samphire), goose greens, fiddleheads, and cow cabbage. Today we are starting to enjoy wild treats again: sumac lemonade and jelly, mushrooms, and juniper berries in gravy.

W Wolves are wild animals with strong hunting and survival instincts. They travel in packs and there are tales of how wolves came close to the pioneer cabins at night, howling and scratching at the door. Wolf tracks in the snow the next morning would show how they had circled the cabins again and again. One settler wrote of their unnerving behavior: "[they were] looking at you between the logs."

X Pioneer parents may have been tired from all their work, but their children would still have found time to play games, such as hopscotch – if they found a level place in the woods – leapfrog, and tag. They would have made mud pies and blown bubbles. Zebediah would have had a bow-and-arrow and a slingshot. He may have even made willow whistles for everyone.

Y After the wool had been gathered, it would be carded (prepared for spinning by being combed out and disentangled with a wooden card), washed, spun into yarn on a spinning wheel, then dyed. (Sometimes pioneers washed the sheep before shearing them.) Finally, yarn would be woven into cloth called homespun or linsey-woolsey, a combination of linen and wool used for clothing and blankets.

Z Names from the past often seem strange to us. You can find them on memorial plaques on church walls, tombstones in cemeteries, and in old books. Many names were taken from the Bible, or were names of qualities parent's might like their children to have, like Honor, Patience, Faith, and Hope. (Parfitt Maggs, Betsy Guppy, and Peppercorn Sanxter are a few I found!)

How many of these things can you find in the paintings?

Aa   acorn, arrow, ark, animals, axe, anvil, amethyst

Bb   blackberries, bush, basket, bonnet, baby, blanket, bear, birch, butterfly, bee, broom, bucket, beaver, beetle, bug

Cc   canoe, corn dolls, coyote, chickadee, chipmunk, chest, cat, candle, cardinal, chestnut

Dd   deer, daredevil, doll, drum, daisy, duck, duckling, dandelion, dragonfly

Ee   eel pie, eggs, embroidery, evergreens, elm trees, eagle

Ff   feather, fish, frog, fir trees, fox, ferns, fence, flag, falcon

Gg   garden, gourds, groundhog, goat, ginseng, gun, gooseberries, grouse, garlic

Hh   hearth, herbs, hoe, hatchet, honey, hat

Ii   infant, iron, icicles, ice skates

Jj   jay, juniper, jug, jack-in-the-box, jewelry, jewelry box

Kk   knitting, knife, kite, kindling, kitten

Ll   logs, ladder, leaves, letter, lake, lynx

Mm   moon, musket, mouse, moccasins, maple syrup, maple leaves

Nn   night sky, nap, nine, newborn

Oo   orchard, oak leaves, owl osprey, oars, otters

Pp   peddler, pipe, pine tree, pine cone, pin needles, powder horn, pan, plow, pack, pail, pie, porcupine, porridge

Qq   quoits, quail, queen

Rr   rain, rushlight, root cellar, roots, rock, robin, rabbit

Ss   spinning wheel, stumps, samplers, skins, skunk, salamander, snail, snake, squirrel

Tt   team, tea, trees, turkeys, turtle, toad

Uu   umbrella, upside down, utensils, unicorn

Vv   vegetables, vulture, vixen

Ww   whippoorwill, wreath, wasp nest, woodpecker, wind

Xx   Xerxes, x-shape

Yy   young, yoke, yawn

Zz   zoo, zebra, zucchini, zero, z-shape